DOWN THE LANE TALES

A STORY, A RHYME
A MOMENT IN TIME
A WISH OR A DREAM
THAT COMES TRUE

by
Christine Harris

Bloomington, IN Milton Keynes, UK

authorHOUSE™

AuthorHouse™
1663 Liberty Drive, Suite 200
Bloomington, IN 47403
www.authorhouse.com
Phone: 1-800-839-8640

AuthorHouse™ UK Ltd.
500 Avebury Boulevard
Central Milton Keynes, MK9 2BE
www.authorhouse.co.uk
Phone: 08001974150

This book is a work of fiction. People, places, events, and situations are the product of the author's imagination. Any resemblance to actual persons, living or dead, or historical events, is purely coincidental.

First published by AuthorHouse 8/1/2006

ISBN: 1-4259-3209-6 (sc)

Printed in the United States of America
Bloomington, Indiana

This book is printed on acid-free paper.

For my husband David who has supported
me day by day and enabled me to do it.

For my two sons James and Simon who have
offered advice and encouragement all the way.

For my mum who knew I could do it!

For all my family who believed I could do it!

ACKNOWLEDGMENTS:

Darin Jewell, my literary agent. Thank you for giving me this opportunity.

Simon Harris. Thank you for your technical support.

TODD THE TADPOLE

Down the lane there was a pond.

Deep down in the dark and murky water a new tadpole had just been born. Along with his brothers and sisters Todd wriggled and splashed his way through the water weeds.

Splish! Splash! Splosh! Todd was happy swimming around his pond. He spent his days wriggling in and out of the water weeds.

2

One day, a silver coin fell into the water. As it sank to the bottom of the pond Todd watched it carefully. It twisted and sparkled as it landed right in front of Todd. It was the prettiest thing Todd had ever seen.

'Perhaps it is a magic coin,' said Todd.

He closed his eyes and wished very hard.

'I wish I had legs,' said Todd, quietly, to the silver coin lying in the sand.

The coin said nothing.

Todd decided to ask it again another day.

In his excitement he almost swam into a net which lay across his path.

'Oops!'

3

A caddis fly grub was hiding in the rocks and he was hungry!

Todd wriggled away quickly out of danger.

'Hello. Where are you going?' Todd asked a very busy water spider.

'I am carrying bubbles of air up into my house made of silk.'

'Would you like a magic coin?' asked Todd. 'I have just seen one fall to the bottom of the pond. It grants wishes you know! You could wish for your house of air to be made, just like that!'

'No. I'd rather do it the old fashioned way thank you. Anyway, I don't believe in magic coins and wishes.'

Todd went on his way.

Over the next few days Todd spent his time wriggling in and out of the water weeds.

'Look out!' called Snail one warm, peaceful afternoon. 'We have a very hungry visitor. You must hide!'

'Another one! Who is it now?' asked Todd

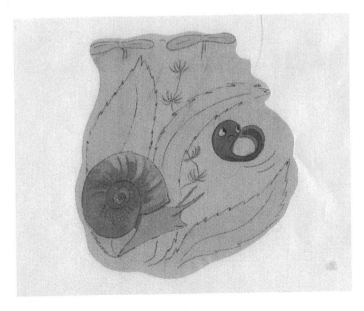

'A great diving beetle,' answered Snail.

'I hope he doesn't take my magic coin,' said Todd with a worried look.

'He won't want that old coin; he just wants a tasty tadpole for his supper!'

'Oh no! I'm going!' declared Todd bravely.

'I don't want to be anyone's supper.'

7

Splish! Splash! Splosh!

Todd went on his way, once more, wriggling in and out of the water weeds.

One day Todd was rushing around as usual and not watching where he was going.

'Oops! Wrong way!' he muttered as he nearly bumped into a stickleback.

'Watch where you're going, kicking all over the place,' grumbled the fish. 'You may have two legs but I have a strong tail and lots of spikes so watch it!'

'Legs? I have legs?'

Up Todd wriggled as fast as he could.

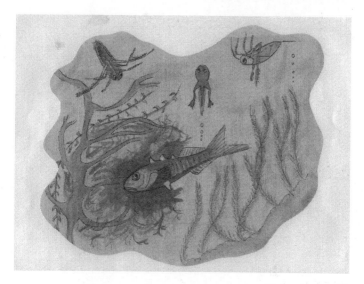

'Oops! Wrong way again!' grinned Todd as he bumped into two water boatmen floating on the surface of the water.

'I have legs!' shouted Todd. 'My magic coin gave me these legs.'

'Just be careful!' they muttered, 'or those legs will get you into bother!'

Some days later, as Todd swam round in his usual manner, something raced past

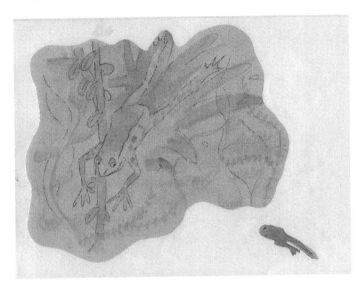

him with the biggest kick and splash Todd had ever seen.

'Croak! Croak!' called 'the someone'. Within minutes he had gone!

'Who was that?' wondered Todd to himself.

The following day Todd swam back to his silver coin lying in the sand.

'Coin,' asked Todd. 'Thank you for my legs; they're lovely, but yesterday I saw someone with four legs and he was able to kick and splash so much better than me. Do you think that you could perhaps give me four legs instead of two?'

The coin said nothing.

'I'll leave you to think about it,' said Todd, feeling very unsure of himself.

Kick! Splish! Splash!

Off went Todd to explore his pond once more. Over the days Todd grew two extra legs and he was so happy.

Todd was now sure that his magic coin was the best friend he could wish for and he was so proud of his four legs that he went to show them to his friend Snail.

Todd hadn't noticed his tail getting shorter; Snail thought that it would be better not to mention it.

As he and Snail chatted together a voice called out nearby. 'Hello! Are you coming to play?'

Todd answered, not knowing who was speaking to him,

'I would like to but...'

'Go on,' urged Snail. 'You can do it. I would have to crawl very slowly up my plant to get to the surface of this pond. With your four legs you could do it in one leap.'

'But what about my coin? I can't do it without my magic wishes.'

'Of course you can,' reassured Snail. You don't need an old coin, even if it is magic. You have grown four long legs which can kick and splash as well as any other creature in this pond. And what's more you did it all by yourself! You don't need magic; you have just got to believe!'

Todd closed his eyes. 'I know I can,' he whispered to himself.

He kicked as hard as he could and made a very little splash.

Then a bigger splash! Then an even bigger splash!

He took a deep breath and with one leap he jumped right out of the pond.

SPLASH!

A shoal of minnows came to see what was happening.

'Where is Todd?' they all called together.

'I'm here! I'm here!' he called. 'I'm out of the pond!'

His new friend sat beside him.

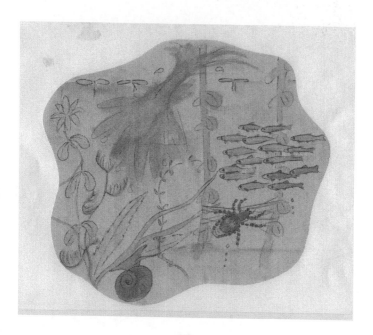

Todd looked down and saw his reflection in the water.

He was so happy.

'I'm a frog,' he whispered and smiled.

As Todd sat in the sunshine and breathed in the fresh air around him, a giggle came from deep inside the pond and a coin twinkled in the murky water as it lay, no longer needed, on the sandy floor.

TIGER WISHES

I have a black and orange tiger cub
That is very dear to me
And though we're very, very happy
There's always something else he'd
rather be.

Sometimes, as we walk down the lane, he looks up at the stars in the sky and makes a wish, a special wish to be a crunching, crawling caterpillar. He likes to think that he could change into a moth and fly into the night sky.

But I say to him:

You are my black and orange tiger cub

Don't wish upon a star

You don't need to be a caterpillar

I love you just the way you are.

Sometimes, on rainy days, he wants to be a parrot flying in the jungle tree tops, showing off his brightly coloured feathers of yellow, red and green.

But I say to him;

You and I play well together

We jump and chase each other all the day

If you were a parrot, I couldn't fly with you

So here on the ground, I'd like you to stay.

Sometimes he wants to change his colours like a chameleon.

Then he could play hide and seek in the long grass and no-one would be able to find him.

But I say to him:

The chameleon's skin is always changing

You have your colours, I have mine

You don't need to mix and match them altogether

Black and orange stripes are yours, and they are fine.

When we cross the road at the zebra crossing he always wants to be a zebra.

He thinks black and white stripes would look fine on a tiger. But I say to him:

There's a pattern for every creature

Stripes and zig-zags, blotches, spots

You may be striped, but in orange and black

So a zebra, you are not.

Even a ladybird does not escape his notice. I think he rather likes the idea of seven big, black spots on his stripy back.

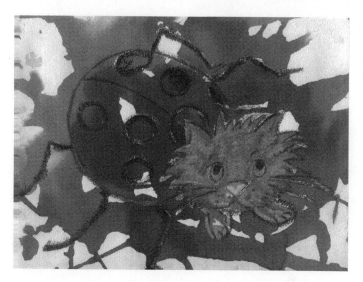

But I say to him:

You have bold stripes, tiger stripes

You wouldn't suit the spots

Your stripes are you, and because you're you,

I love you such a lot.

Sometimes he wants to slither and slide like a snake and hide in lots of different places.

But I say to him...

You are a tiger who can play

And run and leap and crawl

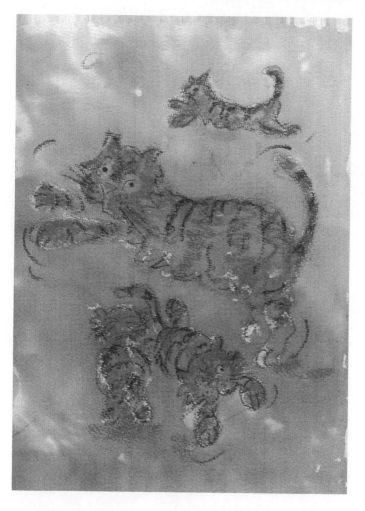

If you were a snake you could slither and slide

But never jump at all.

Just like a snake my tiger cub likes to hide. He hides under a blanket so that no one can see his black and orange stripes anymore.

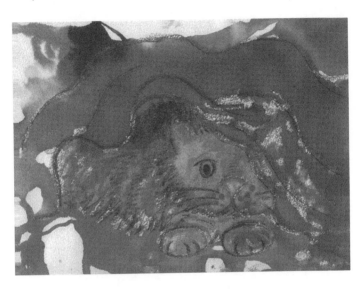

But I say to him:

You're my friend and you're very special

It's what's inside that really counts by far

So stripes, scales, spots and patches don't really matter

Because I love you just the way you are.

Soon, he comes out of hiding...

And when I unzip my tiger's tummy ...

and put on my pyjamas...

my tiger cub wants to be...

just like me!

PICNIC SPIDER

Down the lane we're going for a
picnic

We've packed our basket full of things
to eat.

We have sandwiches and ham

A cake with strawberry jam

And raspberry trifle for a special
treat.

But when I lift the lid and look inside...

I can see a monster in the basket

I close my eyes 'cos I don't want to see

There's a spider oh so hairy

And he looks so very scary

He's sitting in the corner watching

me.

But oh no!

He's wriggling on the corned beef pie!

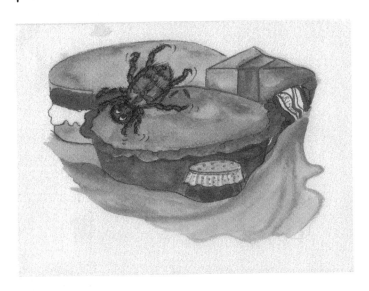

Wow! Look at him dart past the chocolate fingers.

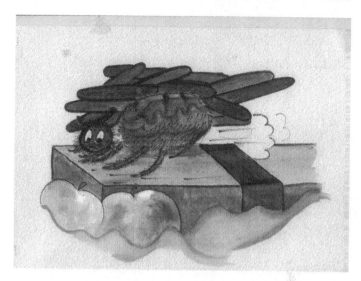

Ooh! He's skating across the raspberry trifle...

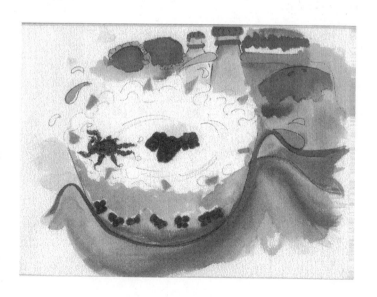

And swinging across the lemonade to the sausage rolls!

Oops! A stumble in the pastry cracks.

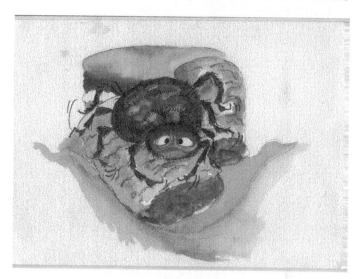

Look out! A scurry up the garlic bread.

Oh dear! He's giving us a long, threatening look on the cucumber sandwiches.

We look through our fingers one by one

I'm hoping that he's tired and fast asleep

As I gasp and stretch my eyes

I am taken by surprise

As I'm feeling brave enough to take a peep.

We are monsters now looking in the basket

The spider can see my friend and me.

A small spider brown and hairy

And not the least bit scary

I am bigger and I know he's watching me.

Then all of a sudden...

He shakes when he sees the large, bulging eyes peering over the lid

He hides from the gale blowing out of

four nostril holes

He jumps and leaps through the air when he sees our gaping mouths quivering

And he runs when gigantic hands grasp for something to chase him away.

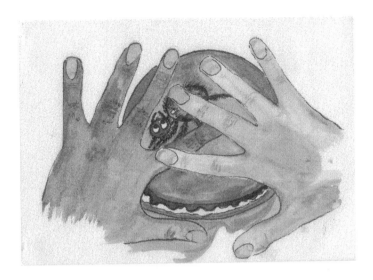

So…….

When I realise who the biggest monster really is I stretch my mouth sideways and smile…

I see a spider running from the basket

A tiny creature as helpless as can be

He is brown and round and hairy

And not the least bit scary

He's going because he is so scared of me.

It's a sunny day and we've enjoyed our picnic

We've shared out all the lovely things
to eat.

We've had sandwiches and ham

A cake with strawberry jam

And trifle covered with tracks of little
feet.

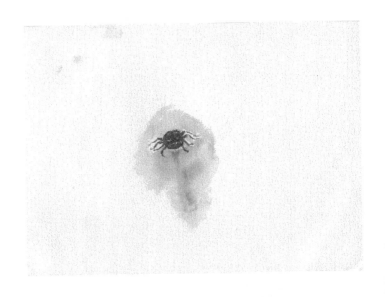

RAINY DAY BOXES

Monday

Down the lane

It's pouring with rain...

'It's pouring with rain

And I can't go out

I'm bored 'cos there's nothing to do'

The weather girl said there'd be black

clouds all week

Rain and possibly snow.

'Mum, what can I do today?'

Asked the little boy in the rain.

And Mum explained as she always did

That they'd fly away in a saucepan lid

To a planet which nobody knew

And eat a huge helping of universe
stew.

They'd share lumps of cheese with the
man in the moon

Who carried it round on a gigantic
spoon.

They'd return to their home tired and
fed

And trundle so wearily, off to their
beds.

Tuesday

'It's Tuesday, it's pouring with rain,

Again!'

'Mum ,what can I do today?'

Asked the little boy in the rain.

'I've built my spaceship from boxes

and glue

I've added the shiny bits, painted it blue

So have you anything else we can do?'

And Mum declared as he knew she would

That they'd put on their waterproofs, pull on their boots

And stomp along pathways that lead to the woods.

'We'll jump in the puddles and make such a splash!

Taking care, not to disturb, the witch in the grass.

She'll be there with her broomstick sneaking around

Checking her blackberries cannot be found.

But you needn't worry, we have blackberries galore

Lying in boxes in our deep freeze store.'

Wednesday

'It's raining and raining again!'

'Mum, what can we do today?'

Asked the little boy in the rain.

And Mum just smiled .

'Today we will

Visit the old castle that stands on the hill.

We'll call to the princess locked up in the tower

And tell her we'll save her in less than an hour.

We'll carry a ladder and climb up with care

To lead the princess down a secret stair

We'll find her a coach made of gold and chrome

Then harness four horses to carry her home.'

Thursday

'It's still raining!'

'Mum, what can we do today?

Asked the little boy in the rain.

Mum said, 'We'll dress up as pirates

And sail across the sea

We'll find a tropical island

And eat pineapples for our tea.

We'll split great big coconuts

And drink the milk inside

We'll eat passion fruit and mangoes

And hunt for treasure at low tide.

We'll find shells and coloured pebbles

And store them in our sack

Then wave and shout from the hilltop

For a ship to carry us back.'

Friday

It rained and it rained

So before he complained

Mum said 'Let us ride

In an old - fashioned train.

We'll thunder down the railway tracks

To there and back again

The trucks will rattle proudly

As they 'chunter' out your name.

The signal will turn red

As the train goes round the bend

The engine will slow down

As we reach our journey's end.'

Saturday

'It's raining again and I can't go out

I'm bored 'cos there's nothing to do!

'What can we do to day?'

Asked the little boy in the rain.

And Mum said 'We're off on a journey

To the shops for food to eat

But we'll sail to the supermarket

In an air balloon, just for a treat.

We'll find a space in the car park

Then go to buy boxes of stuff

We'll load up the basket until it is

full

Checking we've just got enough.

Plenty of cereal, flour and biscuits

Washing powder, apples and leeks

But most important of all, lots of boxes

To use during long, rainy weeks.'

Sunday

Sunday arrived, down came the snow

Granny and Grandpa came over to stay

And the little boy who was bored all week

Went into the garden to play.

And as Grandpa piled snow into a heap

Poor old Mum fell fast asleep!

SEE YOU LATER, EXCAVATOR!

Thump!

Bang!

Bash!

Bump!

Clang!

Clash!

Thump!

Bang!

Bash!

Bump!

Clang!

Clash!

Excavator was tired of breaking things.

He was tired of spoiling everything.

He was tired of everyone covering their ears because he made such a noise.

'This isn't fun,' he moaned to himself. 'I'm going!' Excavator turned his long, metal neck around, arched his shoulders and trundled away, down the lane and off across the fields to the park beyond.

The man with the camera watched him go.

As he wandered along he met a little boy.

'Hello Excavator. You look just like a dinosaur. I'm going to the park. Will you be my dinosaur and come and play?' asked the little boy.

Excavator scooped him up and tossed him in the air.

'Catch me! Catch me!' shouted the little boy. Excavator beamed an extra, excavating smile as he picked him up in his scoop and dropped him again and again.

The man with the camera watched them through his lens.

A few minutes later an old man came along.

'Have you met my dinosaur?' asked the little boy.

The old man cupped his hand over his ear. He couldn't hear the little boy speaking. He looked very sad. He was sad because he couldn't hear the birds in the trees and he couldn't hear the children playing in the schoolyard. He couldn't hear the little boy introduce his dinosaur. Excavator, who was very good at making loud, interesting sounds bellowed and scraped, squealed and growled. The old man beamed from ear to ear.

'I heard that! That was wonderful! It's such a long time since I heard such interesting sounds. Can you make any other sounds?' he asked the excavator as he sat down on a bench nearby.

Excavator trumpeted like an elephant.

He hissed like a snake.

He buzzed like a bee.

'More! More!' shouted the old man.

Excavator squeaked like a mouse.

He squawked like a parrot.

He barked like a dog.

The old man and the little boy clapped their hands.

The man with the camera kept on clicking.

After that, Tom, the park keeper came along with his litter picker.

'So much rubbish! Why don't people ever use the bins?' he grumbled.

'Can I help?' asked Excavator.

Tom nodded wearily as he sat down next to the old man and the little boy. Excavator bent his neck low and scooped up the greasy crisp packets and fizzy pop cans that lay in the long grass. All at once Excavator heard a small, squeaky voice calling for help. He looked down and there was a small, grey mouse with pink ears and twitching whiskers. He looked very anxious.

He was stuck in a greasy, old crisp packet which had been thrown down and left carelessly in the grass verge. Excavator carefully turned the crisp packet upside down and out tumbled a very grateful mouse on to the grass.

The man with the camera got down on his tummy to film the mouse.

At that moment, along came a girl in a wheelchair. She looked up at the towering excavator with a very surprised look on her face.

'Do you like my dinosaur?' asked the little boy.

'I hope he's a plant eater!' she whispered to the little boy. She called to Excavator. 'What's it like to be so tall?'

'I'll show you,' thought Excavator to himself as he lifted the girl out of her chair and high up into the air. She could see over the houses and over the fields and far into the distance. She beamed a big, beaming smile. Excavator carried her for a while so that she could enjoy the ride. After a while he gently put her back in the wheelchair. She pushed herself along, delighted to be with her new friends. The little boy, the old man, Tom, the park keeper and the happy, little mouse skipped along beside her, all enjoying the company of their very own dinosaur.

The man with the camera turned as a very tall, lady came running along the path.

'Hey! Stop that pirate!' she shouted.

Everyone turned to see a clown and a ballet dancer running excitedly with the very tall lady.

Excavator turned his long, metal neck around and grabbed the pirate, giving him a big bite on his bottom. He dangled him in the air and gave him a great, big shake. Excavator dropped him into a rubbish skip standing nearby.

'Oi,' complained the pirate. 'What do you think you're doing?'

The tall lady laughed. The pirate laughed.

The man with the camera pointed his lens at Excavator and the pirate who was, by now, trying to climb out of the skip.

'Wonderful! Wonderful!' he exclaimed as he photographed the whole scene.

Along came a teenage girl wearing blue shorts and a yellow T-shirt. She had a blonde pony tail which bobbed up and down as she walked and in her hand she carried a red and black tennis racquet.

Thwack! She took a ball out of her pocket and hit the ball hard. It flew high into the air and straight into the branches of a tall, beech tree. Excavator turned his long, metal neck around and reached over to the tree. Lifting his scoop high, he shook the branches of the tree and caught the ball, as it fell, with no trouble at all. He carried the ball over to the young lady and bent down to put it carefully in her hand.

'Thank you so much. Will you all help me to practice my tennis?' she asked.

Everyone shouted yes.

The old man threw the ball. The young lady hit it with her tennis racket and Excavator stretched his neck to catch the ball. Tom picked up a banana skin and other litter so that no-one would slip as they played their game.

The girl in the wheelchair, the pirate, the tall lady, and the pantomime horse watched and cheered while the clown and the ballet dancer went to buy some ice-creams for everyone.

The man with the camera kept on clicking.

As they sat in the sunshine enjoying their ice creams, along came Mr Clay, the builder. He was not pleased that his excavator had disappeared. He had come to look for him and tell him to get back to work.

The little boy could tell that his dinosaur didn't want to go back with the builder.

Mr Clay could tell that his excavator didn't want to leave his new friends.

The man with the camera said that they would all be in the newspaper the next day.

He had taken some very good photographs of them playing and laughing, sharing, talking and helping each other. They had shown how important it was to keep the world free from litter and to take care of others. They had been a wonderful advert for the circus which was also a place full of people having fun and laughing together. Just to say thank you the camera man had a free ticket to the circus for everyone.

The new friends all cheered.

Mr Clay had good news for Excavator. He told him that he needed his help to build a new school for the children in the town.

'And what is more, when it is finished,' he said to everyone, 'Excavator is going to retire!'

Excavator didn't say anything; he knew what happened to retired excavators and it wasn't going to be any fun!

Many weeks went by and soon the school was finished. A huge celebration was held in the schoolyard and everyone was invited. The mayor of the town cut the ribbon and declared the new school open.

They played music and games and spent their pennies buying from white elephant stalls. Plants, cakes, jelly, ice cream and hot dogs were on sale to boost school funds and everyone was having a lovely time. That is everyone except Excavator.

The little boy knew why his dinosaur was sad.

The man with the camera was taking pictures of the whole event and he knew why he was sad.

The old man knew, Tom the park keeper knew, the little mouse knew, and the girl in the wheelchair knew. All the people from the circus knew so the teenage tennis player thought she better say something quickly. She had a very important question.

'What will happen to Excavator now that he is retired?' she asked.

Excavator groaned.

Mr Clay sighed.

'Well, ahm...'

'Can we have our dinosaur back again?' asked the little boy eagerly

Mr Clay nodded and smiled.

'Phew. I thought you'd never ask. You certainly can. You can keep him in the school field. He won't need feeding, just a lick of paint now and again to keep his coat shiny and new.'

'Oh thank you, thank you,' said the little boy and the girl in the wheelchair.

'Hooray,' shouted all the children in the schoolyard. 'A new school and a new dinosaur. All in one day!'

The little boy hugged his dinosaur; a big, 'excavator hug' right round his neck.

The school bell rang to end the day
and everyone packed up to go home.

'See you later, Excavator', called Mr Clay as he turned to go.

Thump!

Bang!

Bash!

Bump!

Clang!

Clash!

replied Excavator

and the man with the camera ... clicked!

WEBSTER THE EARTHWORM

Down the lane there was a field and a little earthworm wriggled up into the fresh, cold air. Suddenly three hungry starlings flew down looking for lunch and lunch was a fat, juicy worm.

With a wriggle and a squirm Webster dashed down his tunnel pleased to be back in the dark again.

He stretched and curled his body as he moved onwards, eating the soil as he went.

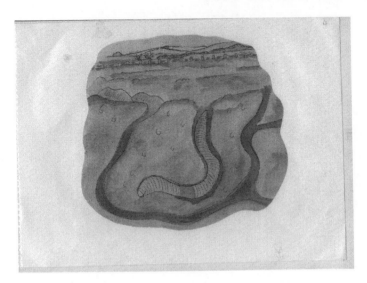

The soil passed right through his body, leaving little piles in Farmer Brown's field.

Farmer Brown smiled a nice, friendly smile.

'Ah, Webster has been here. I can see worm casts in the soil.'

Webster had no ears and he had no eyes but his very special skin could tell him when it was light or dark or when anything or anyone was moving about.

Quickly he had to turn.

Mole was nearby.

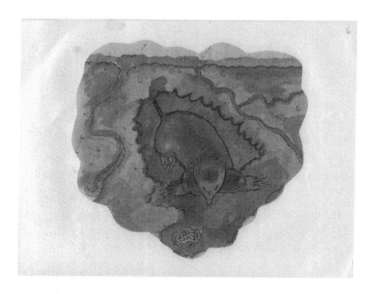

Perhaps he was filling his food cupboard with lots of tasty goodies.

Webster was not going to wait to find out. He didn't want to be tonight's supper.

The rain was falling heavily and getting into Webster's tunnel.

Burrowing upwards he pushed his head out of the soil and grabbed a reddish-brown oak leaf rustling in the breeze.

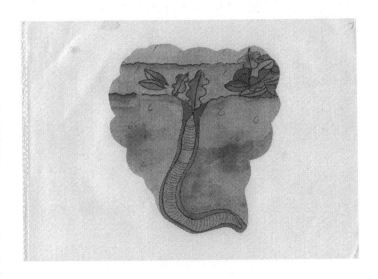

Suddenly he stopped.

Leaves! That meant Autumn was here. It was then that Webster realised he was feeling cold. He needed a few more leaves.

Once more he crawled through his tunnel and pushed his way to the surface.

'Hello,' said Earwig from under a pile of leaves.

Earwig was very happy eating through a small heap of decaying rose petals.

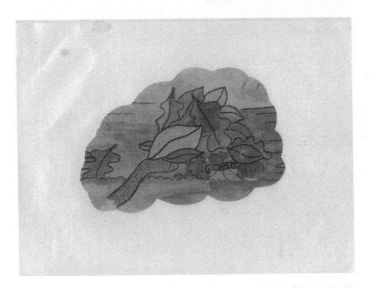

Webster stretched out for some more leaves.

'Help yourself,' whispered a quiet, tired sort of voice.

Webster shook with fear. Another creature that would enjoy an earthworm for supper!

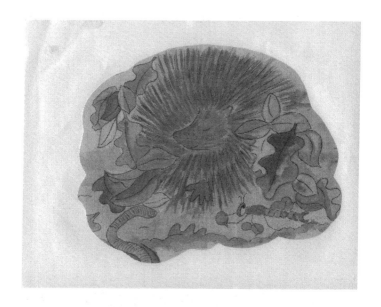

Luckily Hedgehog had eaten his fill and was plump, tired and satisfied.

He was wrapped in a duvet of crinkly leaves and curled up into a ball. He was trying to keep warm in the fallen leaves as he too, was ready for a long, winter sleep.

Earwig looked up! Farmer Brown looked down and smiled.

'Well, it's a good job I noticed you. You nearly ended up in my bag of rubbish. Goodnight little fellows and sleep well. I will see you in the spring.'

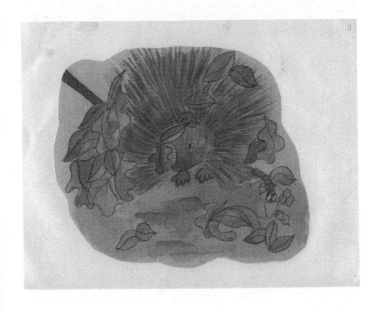

Webster tugged at the leaves, pulling them into his tunnel and blocked

his doorway for the long, cold months ahead.

Curling and stretching, he pushed himself deep into his burrow. Deeper and deeper he went into the dark soil, down into a safe, warm place to curl up for the long, freezing winter.

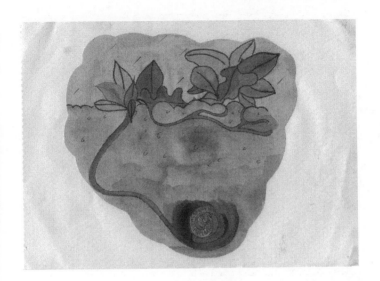

A lovely, dark, warm place to sleep and a place to dream dreams which can come true.

ABOUT THE AUTHOR

Christine Harris is a primary school teacher who has enjoyed sharing her life with hundreds of young people. With a demanding career and a family of her own to support she has been kept busy for many years. She is now determined to realise a career in children's stories, writing and illustrating her own work. This is Christine's first book for young children and she promises it won't be the last!

6910719R00068

Printed in Great Britain
by Amazon.co.uk, Ltd.,
Marston Gate.